The Amazing Wonder Pets

Storybook with Wondertube

P9-DXR-291

Reader's Digest
Children's Books®

Pleasantville, New York • Montréal, Québec • Bath, United Kingdom

Save the Panda

Find these things in the Wondertube:

How do the classroom pets hear from animals in trouble?

Tin-Can Phone

Who are the Wonder Pets going to save?

Baby Panda

School was over for the day, and the classroom pets were relaxing in their homes.

Suddenly the tin-can phone rang. An animal was in trouble!

"It's a baby panda!" said Linny the Guinea Pig, tilting the phone so Ming-Ming Duckling and Turtle Tuck could look inside. "She

More things to discover in the Wondertube:

Box of Scraps

Flyboat

Gong

climbed up that tree to eat bamboo, and now she can't get down."
The Wonder Pets changed into their capes, and put together the Flyboat.

Animal
Fact

Giant pandas have lived in the bamboo forests of China
for millions of years.

Find these things in the Wondertube:

The Wonder Pets flew over green mountains and valleys. Below them the Great Wall of China stretched on and on. Finally they touched down at the edge of a bamboo forest. "Eee! Eee!" squealed the baby panda. Linny's ears perked up. "Walk this way, Wonder Pets!" she said.

What do the Wonder Pets see from the sky?

Great Wall

What kind of trees are in the forest?

Bamboo

More things to discover in the Wondertube:

Linny

Mountains

Bonsai

They made their way through the forest.
"Look!" said Tuck. "That tree is moving!"
The baby panda was at the top.
"We have to get that baby panda down! Any ideas?" asked Linny.

Animal
Fact

Pandas are related to bears—they look like them, have similar skulls
and walk and climb in a similar way. But they are not actually bears!

Find these things in the Wondertube:

Which Wonder Pet suggests they rescue the baby panda using the Flyboat?

Tuck

What do the Wonder Pets make out of bamboo to reach the baby panda?

Ladder

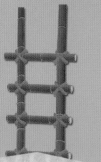

More things to discover in the Wondertube:

Tuck suggested that they try to reach the panda in the Flyboat.

Linny steered expertly, but there was too much bamboo. "We better land, Wonder Pets!" she cried. "Hold on tight!"

The Flyboat landed, and they hopped out.

The baby panda began to cry.

Baby Panda

Linny

"I know! We can make a ladder from bamboo!" said Linny.

Linny passed pieces of bamboo to Tuck, who held them in place as Ming-Ming lashed them to the tree with vines. What a team!

The Wonder Pets helped the panda move from the bamboo tree to the ladder.

The Wonder Pets helped the panda climb down the ladder.

"We got her!" cried Linny.

Animal Fact

Giant pandas are only about the size of a stick of butter at birth. They don't open their eyes until they are 6 to 8 weeks old, and they do not move around until 3 months.

Find these things in the Wondertube:

Who come to find the baby panda?

Mama Panda

What do the Wonder Pets eat to celebrate?

Celery

More things to discover in the Wondertube:

"Look! It's her mama!" said Ming-Ming.
The baby panda ran into Mama Panda's arms and hugged her tightly.
"Oh, thank you, Wonder Pets!" said the Mama Panda. "I was so worried!"
"You're welcome, Mama Panda!" said Tuck.

Soy Sauce

Ming-Ming

"This calls for some celery!" said Linny, pulling out a stick.

"Celery is very good with soy sauce!" said the Mama Panda, handing them a bottle.

The baby panda reached for the celery. "Eee?"

"I don't think so, baby," said the Mama Panda. "You've had more than enough to eat today!"

Animal Fact

Giant pandas eat 20 to 40 pounds of bamboo each day. To get this much food, a panda spends most of the day finding food and eating. The rest of its time is spent sleeping and resting. Pandas get much of the water they need from bamboo.

Find these things in the Wondertube:

Save the Penguin

How do the classroom pets find out about animals in trouble?

Tin-can Phone

What baby animal is caught on an iceberg?

Baby Penguin

More things to discover in the Wondertube:

"Ring! Ring!" It was the tin-can phone, and the classroom pets knew what that meant.

"There's an animal in trouble!" called out Ming-Ming Duckling. Linny the Guinea Pig picked up the phone.

"Squawk! Squawk!" came a sound from inside.

Linny

Iceberg

"It's a baby penguin," said Linny. "He's caught on an iceberg!"
"We have to help him!" said Turtle Tuck.
After changing into their capes, they put together the Flyboat.
"Hop in!" said Linny. "We've got a baby penguin to save!"

Animal
Fact

Unlike most birds, penguins aren't able to fly. They are great swimmers though!
When they are in the water, they dive and flap their wings. It looks like they are flying.

Find these things in the Wondertube:

What animal do the Wonder Pets see from the sky at the South Pole?

Whale

What do the Wonder Pets travel in to reach the iceberg?

Rowboat

More things to discover in the Wondertube:

Soon the Wonder Pets were flying over ice and snow. Below them they saw a whale with a baby. They also saw some seals.

"Here we are, Wonder Pets!" Linny cried as the Flyboat skidded to a stop. "The South Pole! Now let's find that baby penguin!"

Tuck pointed to some tracks in the snow. The Wonder Pets followed the tracks until they came to a patch of slippery ice. They

Tuck

Ming-Ming

passed a rowboat and arrived at the water's edge.

Linny pointed to a small floating iceberg with the baby penguin on it. He couldn't swim!

The Wonder Pets got into the rowboat and put on life vests. Linny rowed, but the wind was very strong. Ming-Ming flapped her wings hard. Tuck kicked his feet in the water behind the boat. What a team!

Animal Fact

Penguins huddle shoulder to shoulder to keep warm. Their feathers have a special oil to help make them waterproof and windproof.

Find these things in the Wondertube:

What does Linny put on the baby penguin to help him float?

Life Vest

Who is waiting on the shore for the baby penguin?

Mama and Papa Penguin

More things to discover in the Wondertube:

"Squawk!" called the baby penguin.
The Wonder Pets saw that the iceberg had split in two.
"Hang on, baby penguin!" called Tuck.
The penguin was struggling to keep his balance. Just as he was about to fall, Linny caught him. She put a life vest on the baby penguin, and they headed back to shore.

 **Ming-Ming**

 **Polar Bear**

They found the penguin's parents waiting. The baby penguin rushed over to them.

"Oh, thank you, Wonder Pets!" cried the mother penguin.

"You're welcome, Mama Penguin!" said Linny. "This calls for some celery!"

Animal Fact

Penguin parents take turns sitting on their egg. First, the daddy sits while the mommy searches for food, and when she comes back, it's daddy's turn to explore the ice.

Find these things in the Wondertube:

Save the Dinosaur

What baby animal is caught between two leaning rocks?

Triceratops

What does Linny use to fix the Flyboat's squeaky wheels?

Oil Can

More things to discover in the Wondertube

"Bye!" the children called out to their classroom pets as they left for the day. Soon after they'd gone, the tin-can phone rang.

"There's an animal in trouble!" said Ming-Ming Duckling as she flew over.

Turtle Tuck scampered up from the sink to join her.

Linny the Guinea Pig picked up the phone and heard a loud, "Hoonk! Hoonk!"

"It's a baby dinosaur!" Linny cried. Inside the phone they saw a baby Triceratops stuck between two leaning rocks.

Linny

Tin-Can Phone

"Let's save the Triceratops!" the three of them sang out together. Holding hands, they jumped into a box of scraps. They popped up wearing their capes.

Quickly, the Wonder Pets put together the Flyboat. They noticed the wheels were squeaking. Linny squirted oil on them, and the friends were ready to roll!

Animal Fact

Triceratops dinosaurs were herbivores, or plant eaters. They used their beaklike mouths and powerful jaws to eat low-lying plants.

Find these things in the Wondertube:

The Flyboat makes a bumpy landing down the spine of what animal?

Alamosaurus

What kind of animal lands on the rock?

Pterodactyl

"Let's go, Wonder Pets, we have a baby dinosaur to save!" said Linny. Tuck noticed a dinosaur poster hanging on the classroom wall. They flew toward the poster . . . and found themselves in an amazing prehistoric world.

"Gooo, Wonder Pets! Yaaayyy!" they cheered.

Below them, the Wonder Pets saw dinosaurs of all shapes and sizes. They made a bumpy landing down the spine of an Alamosaurus.

More things to discover in the Wondertube

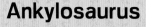 **Ankylosaurus**

Trees

They hurried toward the leaning rocks—and slipped in a mud patch!

"Cool! Slippin' and a' slidin' in the slime!" the Wonder Pets sang.

"Hoonk!" It was the baby Triceratops. There was a large rock over his head. Just then a prehistoric bird landed on the rock.

"That pterodactyl will make the rock fall on the Triceratops!" Tuck cried.

Animal Fact

Triceratops lived a long, long time ago – well before people or guinea pigs or ducklings.

Find these things in the Wondertube:

What teeters on the edge of the cliff?

Rock

Who shows up after the Wonder Pets save the baby dinosaur?

Daddy Dino

More things to discover in the Wondertube:

The Wonder Pets had an idea.

Linny squirted mud into the crack between the rocks to make the dinosaur slippery. "Ming-Ming, you pull on the middle horn," she said. "Tuck, you push on the dinosaur's backside."

With teamwork, the Wonder Pets eased the Triceratops out from between the rocks.

"Look out!" Tuck shouted.

They moved out of the way just as the rock came crashing down.

Ming-Ming

Tuck

Tuck gave the baby dinosaur a hug. The dinosaur gave Tuck a sloppy kiss.

"Thank you, Wonder Pets! You saved my little baby!" cried the father Triceratops.

"You're welcome, daddy dinosaur!" said Linny.

Animal Fact

Triceratops ran as fast as a car.

Save the Sea Turtle

Find these things in the Wondertube:

What baby animal just hatched on a beach?

Baby Sea Turtle

What do the classroom pets change into to become Wonder Pets?

Capes

"The phone is ringing!" Linny the Guinea Pig called out to the other classroom pets. She dropped down through the trapdoor beneath her food dish.

"There's an animal in trouble somewhere!" Turtle Tuck said. Ming-Ming Duckling flew over to join them.

Inside the tin-can phone, the classroom pets saw a baby sea turtle . . . who couldn't find the sea.

"Goo ga!" the newly hatched baby sea turtle babbled. The remains of her broken shell were scattered around her.

More things to discover in the Wondertube

Blossoms

Tin-Can Phone

"She needs to get to the ocean, but she can't find it!" said Linny. "Let's help the sea turtle!"

The classroom pets joined hands and leaped off the shelf into a box of scraps. They popped up wearing their capes. There was only one thing left to do—build the Flyboat!

Animal Fact

Sea turtles feed on sea grasses. Green sea turtles are named for the color of their body.

Find these things in the Wondertube:

Who was swimming out to sea?

Sister Turtles

Which Wonder Pet tries to turn around the baby sea turtle by picking her up?

Ming-Ming

More things to discover in the Wondertube:

The Wonder Pets flew over the rocky coast of Japan, touching down on the baby sea turtle's beach. Three little sea turtles were making their way toward the sea.

"They must be the baby sea turtle's sisters!" said Linny.

Sushi

Tempura

But the baby sea turtle was walking away from the ocean.

Ming-Ming picked up the baby sea turtle. "We can bring her back to the ocean!"

"Put the baby sea turtle down!" said Tuck. "She has to learn to get to the ocean by herself."

Animal Fact

Sea turtles don't come on land, except when mommy sea turtles need to lay eggs.

Find these things in the Wondertube:

What do the Wonder Pets use to build a path for the baby sea turtle?

Seashells

What tells the Wonder Pets it's starting to get dark outside?

Moon

More things to discover in the Wondertube

Ming-Ming put the turtle down. "But it's dark!" she cried.
"We've got to think of something fast," said Linny.
"Why don't we make a path to the ocean for the baby sea turtle?" suggested Tuck.

Ming-Ming

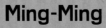

Seashell

Together the Wonder Pets arranged some shiny seashells to create a path. What a team!

"Teamwork meets roadwork!" said Ming-Ming.

Animal Fact

Sea turtles can stay underwater a long, long time without coming up for air. To conserve oxygen, their hearts can slow to one beat every nine minutes.

Find these things in the Wondertube:

Who is waiting in the water for the baby sea turtle?

Turtles

Who is waving good-bye to the Wonder Pets?

Baby Sea Turtle

More things to discover in the Wondertube:

The baby sea turtle made her way to the water's edge, where she was greeted by her sisters. "Goo! Gaa!" they said. "Goo! Goo!" the baby sea turtle replied.

Tuck

Flyboat